N

War Lord's Castle

Giant's Castle

MAP OF TASHI'S
VILLAGE AND SURROUNDS

Seaport

Emperor's
Palace

Tashi

Tashi

written by
Anna Fienberg
and **Barbara Fienberg**

illustrated by
Kim Gamble

ALLEN&UNWIN
SYDNEY•MELBOURNE•AUCKLAND•LONDON

Anna Fienberg would like to thank the Literature Board of the Australia Council for their assistance.

This collection first published by Allen & Unwin in 2020

Allen & Unwin
83 Alexander Street
Crows Nest NSW 2065 Australia
Phone: (61 2) 8425 0100
Email: info@allenandunwin.com
Web: www.allenandunwin.com

 A catalogue record for this book is available from the National Library of Australia

ISBN 978 1 76052 544 6

For teaching resources, explore www.allenandunwin.com/resources/for-teachers

Cover and text design by Sandra Nobes
Set in 13 pt Horley Old Style
This book was printed in January 2020 by Hang Tai Printing Company Limited, China

10 9 8 7 6 5 4 3 2 1

www.tashibooks.com

TASHI
and the SILVER CUP

In a land far away, there was once a family who longed for a baby. Yet years passed and no baby arrived, and the wife grew thin and silent.

Now in the village there lived a wise and kindly man who had studied medicine and magic potions all his life. When villagers had sore knees or an aching head, a worrying cough or sadness that stayed too long, they went to see him. 'He'll know just what to do,' they said, and even as they watched him mix his herbs and pour his potions, they began to feel better.

And so, after still another childless year had passed, the wife's mother made up her mind. Finding her daughter sobbing into her

breakfast one morning, she said, 'Why don't we pay a visit to Wise-as-an-Owl and ask him for help?'

Off they went that very day. They knocked at his door and while they waited, they marvelled at its mysterious carvings of dragons and birds and lotus flowers, and were filled with hope.

Wise-as-an-Owl listened carefully to the wife. He nodded, smiling, as he turned the pages of his great Book of Knowledge that lived in his study.

'I think this mixture will do the trick,' he told them, taking down several bottles and mixing their ingredients in a bowl.

The wife danced all the way home and that night as she sipped the strangely delicious mixture, the family toasted her, their voices ringing through the house with excitement and laughter.

And they weren't disappointed: within the year a baby was born.

He was given the name Tashi. The whole village took a great interest in his birth and watched him closely to see if this child would be special in any way.

He certainly was a lively baby, always crawling into small spaces and high places.

'He's so curious,' his father said fondly. 'Yesterday I found him in the grandfather clock, trying to find out what made it tick.'

'He's quick as a firecracker,' his mother said tiredly. 'It's always Tashi who's first to the door when someone calls.'

And so it was that when half the village turned up to celebrate his first birthday, his mother put him firmly into his high chair to keep him out of mischief. But Tashi made sure that he was right in the middle of the room and the noise and the fun.

The presents were put on a large table and all exclaimed in admiration when they saw the beautiful silver cup that Wise-as-an-Owl had brought. His son, Much-to-Learn, put it into Tashi's tiny hands.

'Happy birthday, Tashi,' said Much-to-Learn. And the young man smiled, gazing at his father's silver cup fondly. 'This cup has had a very special place in our family, Tashi. Keep it safe.'

People came and went all afternoon, and there were great bowls of spicy fish and tasty noodles, duck eggs and gooseberries. Third Aunt played her violin and Luk Ahead the fortune teller wept with joy for the beauty of it. Much-to-Learn performed the magic tricks he'd been practising all week, and didn't make one mistake.

Finally, the food was all eaten, the wine and tea drunk, and the toasts were made. 'Three cheers for little Tashi!' the guests all cheered together.

People were beginning to say goodbye when someone noticed: the silver cup was gone!

A shocked hush swept over the room.

'But how could this happen?' cried Tashi's mother. 'It couldn't just vanish, could it?'

'Was this one of your magic tricks, Much-to-Learn?' Tashi's grandma asked.

'No!' he replied hotly. 'Sometimes I don't, well, get things quite right, but I would never, *ever* use the silver cup just to do a trick.'

Grandma nodded and patted his cheek, and they joined the search. People looked under chairs, behind the cupboards, and even into the garden outside. Such a hunting and scurrying and poking about went on, and still the cup couldn't be found.

But little bright-eyed Tashi had been watching from his chair.

He had seen someone pick up the cup and drop it on the floor.

He had watched this person casually kick it under a sofa and then sit down above it.

He had seen him drop his cap to cover the cup and then pocket the cap and cup together. Tashi's bright black eyes had not missed a thing.

Now, when everyone had given up the search in despair, Tashi called to be lifted from his chair. Scrambling down, he tottered and crawled across the room to his uncle Tiki Pu.

Tiki Pu looked very embarrassed when Tashi pulled at his trouser pocket, and he tried to move away. But Tashi clamped both arms around his leg and hung on. Tiki Pu shook his leg, but Tashi was stuck fast.

People laughed, at first.

'Tashi looks just like my puppy clinging to the broom when I'm trying to sweep the floor!' said Mrs Ping.

But they stopped laughing and turned to stare when Tashi tipped the cup out of Tiki Pu's pocket.

'Well I never saw such a thing!' and 'Who would have thought?' and 'Shame!' could be heard throughout the room.

Tiki Pu blushed fiery red. 'I can't imagine

how that cup could possibly have got in there,' he said. 'Someone must have knocked it into my pocket.'

And for the sake of ending the party on a happy note, people pretended to believe him.

But when all the guests had gone home, Grandma scooped Tashi up and hugged him. 'What a clever little Tashi!' she cried.

From that day on, although everyone in the village went on doing exactly what they always did, and life continued in the way it always had, people knew that with Tashi, something quite wonderful had arrived in the world.

TASHI

'I have a new friend,' said Jack one night at dinner.

'Oh, good,' said Mum. 'What's his name?'

'Tashi, and he comes from a place very far away.'

'That's interesting,' said Dad.

'Yes,' said Jack. 'He came here on a swan.'

'A black or white swan?' asked Dad.

'It doesn't *matter*,' said Jack. 'You always ask the wrong questions!'

'How did Tashi get here on a swan then?' asked Mum.

'Well,' said Jack, 'it was like this. Tashi's parents were very poor. They wanted to come to this country, but they didn't have enough money for the airfare. So they had to sell Tashi to a war lord to buy the tickets.'

'How much did the tickets cost?' said Dad.

'It doesn't *matter*,' said Jack. 'You always ask the wrong questions!'

'So why is Tashi here, and not with the war lord?' asked Mum.

'Well,' said Jack, 'it was like this. Soon after Tashi's mother and father left, he was crying for them down by the lake. A swan heard his cries and told him to jump on his back. The swan flew many days and nights until he arrived here, right at the front door of Tashi's parents' new house.'

'Did he arrive in the morning or the afternoon?' asked Dad.

'It doesn't *matter*,' said Jack. 'And I'm not telling you any more because I'm going to bed.'

A week passed and Jack ate lunch with
Tashi every day. And every day he heard a
marvellous adventure.

He heard about the time Tashi found a ring
at the bottom of a pond, and when he put it on
his finger he became invisible.

He heard about the time Tashi met a little woman as small as a cricket, and she told him the future.

And he heard about the time Tashi said he wanted a friend just like Jack, and *look!* the fairy had granted his wish.

But at the end of the week he heard the best
adventure of all.

'Listen to what happened to Tashi yesterday,'
Jack said to Mum and Dad at dinner.

'Last night there was a knock at Tashi's
door and when he opened it, guess who was
standing there!'

'Who?' said Mum.

24

'The war lord, come to take Tashi back! Tashi turned and ran through the house and out the back door into the garden. He hid under the wings of the swan.'

'Go on,' said Mum.

'Well, the angry war lord chased him out
into the night and when he found the swan he
shouted, "Where did young Tashi go?"

'The swan answered, "If you want to find
Tashi, you must go down to the pond. Drop
this pebble into the water, and when the ripples
are gone you will see where Tashi is hiding."'

27

'Did the war lord find the pond?' asked
Mum.

'Well,' said Jack, 'it was like this. The war
lord did as the swan told him and dropped the
pebble into the pond. But when the water was
still again, he didn't see Tashi. Instead he saw
his own country, and his own palace, and he
saw all his enemies surrounding it, preparing
to attack.

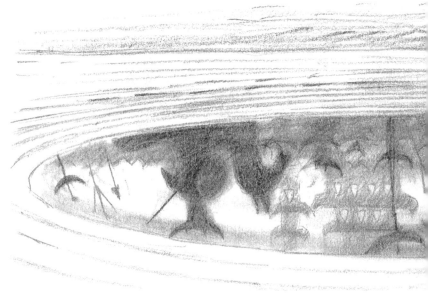

'The war lord was very upset by what he'd seen in the pond, and he said to the swan, "I must go home at once!"

"'I will take you," said the swan. "Just climb on my back." And bending his head under his wing, he whispered, "Goodbye Tashi, I am homesick for my country. Just stay in the long grass, and he won't see you. Goodbye."'

'Can I bring Tashi home tomorrow to play?'
asked Jack.

'Oh, yes,' said Mum and Dad. 'We're dying
to meet Tashi.'

32

Jack and Tashi sat at the kitchen table, drinking their juice.

'Would you like to play in the garden now?' asked Mum.

'Oh, yes!' said Tashi. 'I like gardens.'

'We could look for a dragon to kill,' Jack said
hopefully to Tashi.

'Are there any dragons left in the
garden?' asked Dad.

'You *always* say the wrong thing!' said Jack.

'He's right though,' said Tashi as they closed
the door behind them. 'There aren't any
dragons left in the whole world. Can you guess
how I know?'

'How?' asked Jack.

'Well, it was like this. Come and I'll tell you about the time I tricked the last dragon of all.'

DRAGON BREATH

Jack took Tashi outside to the peppercorn tree. They climbed up to Jack's special branch and when they were sitting comfortably, Jack said, 'Did you really meet a dragon?'

'Yes', said Tashi, 'it was like this. One day
Grandma asked me to go to the river to catch
some fish for dinner.'

'Was this in your old country?' asked Jack.

'Of course,' said Tashi. 'Grandma doesn't
believe in travel.

'Anyway, before I set off, Grandma warned
me, "Whatever you do, Tashi," she said,
"don't go near the steep, crumbly bank at the
bend of the river. The edge could give way and
you could fall in. And," she added, "keep your
eyes open for dragons."'

'*Dragons!*' said Jack. 'What do you do if you
meet a dragon?'

'Well, it was like this,' said Tashi. 'I walked
across the field to the river and I caught five
fish for dinner. I was just putting them into
a couple of buckets of water to keep them fresh
when I saw a cloud of smoke. It was rising
from a cave, further up the mountain.'

'Ooah, did you run away home?' asked Jack.

'Not me,' said Tashi. 'I took my buckets and climbed up the mountain and there, sitting at the mouth of the cave, was the biggest dragon I'd ever seen.'

'Have you seen many?' asked Jack.

'I've seen a few in my time,' said Tashi. 'But not so close. And *this* dragon made me very cross.

47

'He was chomping away at a crispy, dragon-breath-roasted pig.

'"That's my father's pig you're eating," I said.

'"I don't care," said the dragon. "I needed something to cheer me up."

"'You can't eat other people's pigs just because you feel like it," I told him.

"'Yes, I can. That's what dragons do."

'So I sat down next to him
and said, "Why do you
need cheering up?"

'"Because I'm lonely," said the dragon.
"There was a time when I had a huge noisy
family. We'd spend the days swooping over the
countryside, scaring the villagers out of their
wits, stealing pigs and geese and grandfathers,
and roasting them with our dragon breath.

"'Then we'd sing and roar all night till the sun came up. Oh, those were the days!" The dragon sighed then and I moved back a bit. "But Mum and Dad grew old and died, and I ate up the rest of the family. So now I'm the only dragon left."

'He looked straight at me and his scaly dragon eyes grew slitty and smoky. "A few mouthfuls of little boy might make me feel better," he said.'

'Oh no!' said Jack. 'What happened then?'

'Well, it was like this. I quickly stood up, ready to run, and the water in my buckets slopped out over the side.

"'Look out!' cried the dragon. "Watch your step! Dragons don't like water, you know. We have to be careful of our fire.'"

'*Aha!*' said Jack.

'Yes,' said Tashi. 'That gave me an idea.
So I looked him in the eye and said, "You're
not the last dragon, oh no you're not! I saw one
only this morning down by the river. Come,
I'll show you, it's just by the bend."

'Well, the dragon grew all hot with
excitement and he followed me down the
mountain to the bend in the river. And there it
was, all steep and crumbly.

'"He can't be here," said the dragon, looking
around. "Dragons don't go into rivers."

'"This one does," I said. "Just look over the
edge and you'll see him."

'The dragon leaned over and peered down
into the water. And he saw another dragon!

'He breathed a great flaming breath. And the
other dragon breathed a great flaming breath.

'He waved his huge scaly wing. And the
other dragon waved his huge scaly wing.

'And then the steep crumbly bank gave way
and *whoosh!* the dragon slid *splash!* into the
river.

'An enormous dragon-shaped cloud of steam rose up from the river, and the water sizzled as the dragon's fire was swallowed up.'

'Hurray!' said Jack. 'And then did you run away home?'

'Yes,' said Tashi. 'I certainly did run home because I was late.

'And sure enough Grandma said, "Well, you took your time catching those fish today, Tashi."'

'So that's the end of the story,' said Jack sadly. 'And now all the village was safe and no one had to worry any more.'

'Well, it wasn't quite like that,' said Tashi.
'You see, the dragon had just one friend. It was
Chintu the giant, and he was as big as two
houses put together.'

'*Oho!*' said Jack. 'And Chintu is for
tomorrow, right?'

'Right!' said Tashi.

And the two boys slipped down
from the tree and wandered
back into the house.

KIDNAPPED!

Jack came in the door and flopped down on the sofa. Dad sprawled out next to him. 'Next time we're invited to your Aunty Fullpot's,' he groaned, throwing the keys onto the table, 'I'm going to say we're busy. And as usual, I ate far too much!'

'Me too,' said Mum, coming to sit on his knee. 'I had to keep my mouth busy with pavlova, otherwise when she started complaining about Jack's hair I would have said something rude.'

'Like what?' said Jack, looking up.

Mum shrugged. 'Ever since I was little, Aunty Fullpot's made me itch with irritation. Look, I'm coming out in hives.'

Dad nodded. 'Who does she think she is?
Judge Fullpot? Always criticising, sneering at
my socks just because they're different colours.
I told her I wear them like that on *purpose*,
but she just kept frowning at them like they
were a couple of cockroaches.'

'Oh well,' said Mum. 'I'm sure lots of
families have at least one difficult relative.'

'Yes,' said Jack. 'Do you remember Tashi's
Uncle Tiki Pu?'

'How could we ever forget?' said Dad,
sitting up.

'Well, you should hear the worst thing he did.'

'We *should*!' cried Dad, his bottom leaping up and down on the couch with excitement.

'I'll make us a cup of tea to go with it,' said Mum.

'And can we have that apple cake from yesterday?' said Jack. '*You* might have had second helpings at Aunty Fullpot's, but I was outside sweeping the path and washing the windows.'

'You made a lucky escape,' said Dad, 'I'll tell you that for free.'

When they were settled comfortably, Jack began. 'Well, it was like this. Tashi and Lotus Blossom had been practising their tightrope act for the end-of-year concert.'

'I didn't know Tashi could walk a tightrope,' said Mum.

'As well as walk through walls,' added Dad.

'They're not the same *thing*,' said Jack.
'Tashi says being a good tightrope walker
hasn't got anything to do with magic. It's
practice. And he reckoned he needed a lot of
that. Plus peace and quiet. Anyway, as he and
Lotus Blossom were plodding up the path, all
tired out from practising, they heard angry
voices coming from the kitchen.

'Tashi sighed. "That will be Grandma and
Tiki Pu. There's always shouting in our house
now that Tiki Pu has come back to live with
us."

Mum and Dad looked at each other in horror.

'Yes,' said Jack. 'Lotus Blossom couldn't understand it either. "Why did your parents agree to him moving back in with them when they know all the trouble he causes?"'

'Tashi gave another, bigger sigh. "It's because he's been making even more trouble for everyone else in the village – even the *Baron*. It seems he was supposed to sell some turtles for the Baron at a good price, but instead of handing over the money, he kept half of it for himself. Now no one will give him any work or have anything more to do with him; and on top of that he has to pay back the money he cheated from the Baron. The Baron's been saying if he doesn't give it back by next week, he thinks that a very nasty accident will happen to Tiki Pu."

'"Wah!" said Lotus Blossom. "But how can he possibly find the money if no one will give him any work?"

'Tashi held up his hands. "Just what I want to know. Still, it's not our problem, thank goodness."'

'Well, I don't know about that,' Dad put in, 'family is family...'

'Yes, but how much do you have to put up with?' said Mum. 'Remember the time Tiki Pu—'

'Can I get on with the story? Well, when Tashi walked in the door, Grandma was still banging pots about. "What did he do this time Grandma?"

'Grandma snorted. "Oh, Tashi! You saw the Eight Treasures rice dish I spent the whole morning cooking? Well, I just slipped out to the garden for one minute and when I came back there was Tiki Pu cramming the last spoonful into his mouth!"

"'Oh no! That was for Third Aunt because she's been sick, wasn't it?"

"'Yes, it was. Not that Tiki Pu would care. He thinks I like to spend my time cooking just in case he should feel hungry when he comes by. That man thinks of no one but himself." And she banged another saucepan.

'Just as Tashi was getting into bed that night, Tiki Pu appeared outside his window. "Tashi! Put on your coat and shoes and come out here. I want to show you something."

'Tashi groaned when he saw the snow was falling but he was curious, too, so he did as he was told.

'"What is it?" he asked, as a bag was dropped over his head and two strong arms wrapped around him. He felt himself being carried bumpily, and dropped into a cart that was waiting in the road behind the house. He kicked and tried to call out but the bag was tied tightly over his mouth. The cart and horse moved off straightaway, and Tashi lay in darkness, shivering.

'The hessian bag smelled of herrings, and Tashi began to gag. He tried to pull at the ties but it was no use. Little pinpricks of light stabbed through – moonlight sparkling on snow, a cooking fire in the forest... But he couldn't make out where they were headed. He tried to take a deep breath from his belly to calm himself, but the greasy stink of fish nearly choked him.

'At last he sensed someone move through the darkness and the bag was pulled from his head. He wiped his eyes and looked about him. They were on a dark and lonely road. The snow had stopped but it was cold enough

to freeze his nose and ears. The only light in
the world was the lantern tied to the cart.
It showed Tiki Pu sitting beside him.

"'Tiki Pu! What are you doing? Where are
we going?"

'Tiki Pu frowned. "I don't like it any more
than you do, Tashi, but you must see that I
really don't have any choice. The Baron says
that he will punish me if I don't pay back

the money I stole from him and this seems to be the only way I can do it. I'm afraid I've arranged to sell you to General Zeng. Oh, and I've packed your magic shoes. You know, with all this magic at your fingertips you're really worth quite a lot of money."

"'But I'm your nephew! You can't sell me to General Zeng. Everyone knows how cruel he is. What about our family, how sad they will be if I disappear."

"'Yes, it's a great pity," said Tiki Pu,
"but I'll miss my comfortable bed and your
grandmother's cooking too, Tashi, so you see
it's just as hard for me. I've thought and thought
and you are the only thing I have to sell."

Tashi stared at Tiki Pu in wonder. He
started to say he wasn't Tiki Pu's to sell, that
he didn't even know how he could be *related*
to such a mean, selfish snake of a man ... but
he closed his lips tight. Useless.

'Tiki Pu patted his shoulder. "That's it,
you understand. Oh, I haven't been sleeping
at all well, tossing around all night with this
problem nagging at me. But now I've thought

of this plan, everything will be all right. Such a relief, you know." And he sighed contentedly.

'When they arrived at General Zeng's castle, Tashi and Tiki Pu were taken to the Great Hall. Marble statues lit by tall candles stood like guards around the walls. Tashi watched their shadows shuddering across the vast floor as the grand doors closed behind them.

'The first thing the General did was to take Tashi's magic shoes. Then he marched over to his small son, Long Awaited, and placed them at his feet. "Here," said the General, "put these on and let's see you jump up and touch the ceiling." Servants and guards crept in to see, whispering together behind their hands.

'But oh no, as soon as Long Awaited took a step, the shoes fell off.

'"Stupid boy," shouted the General, red in the face. "Can't you walk properly?"

'"The shoes are too big," wailed Long Awaited.

'"Stuff the toes with your stockings then," the General ordered.

'A servant ran forward and it was soon done. But a sigh of disappointment rose around the room when the boy's jump was no higher than usual.

'The General's face grew dark with rage and he turned on Tiki Pu. "These aren't the magic shoes. You have lied to me!" He drew his sword.

'Tashi lifted his voice. "The shoes are only magic when they are on my feet, my lord. Look, let me show you." He slipped them on and leapt, quick as a firefly, up the wall and across the ceiling.

'Everyone gasped in wonder but the
General growled, "What good is that to me?"
Then a thoughtful look stole over his face,
and he put his sword back in its sheath. He
studied Tashi for a moment or two, as if
weighing something up. At last, to Tashi's
relief, he said, "Now, Tashi, your job will be
to keep my son amused and out of mischief."

He chuckled proudly. "His nurse can't keep up with him anymore. Take Tashi to your room," he said to his son as he led Tiki Pu away.

'Upstairs, over in the east wing of the castle, Tashi faced Long Awaited. Was he to be this boy's slave forever? Could he escape? But there was no time to think of a plan now. Long Awaited took a running jump at him, playfully cuffing him on the shoulder.

"'Well," said Tashi, "tell me, what do you most like to do?"

"'I like fighting and running and jumping and playing tricks on people."

'Tashi looked out the window. "It's snowing again, and still dark. Perhaps you would like to hear a story instead? I've had quite a few running and jumping adventures in my time."

'Long Awaited wasn't sure he wanted to hear any stories at first but in a very short time he was sitting, mouth open, lost in

Tashi's world. Just think, no one had ever told him a story before.'

Dad shivered. 'Now *that's* scary.'

'The next few days with Long Awaited were not easy for Tashi. The boy was used to taking what he wanted and doing whatever he wanted. He certainly expected to win every game they played, and kicked Tashi if ever he should dare to run too fast or catch too many balls.

'At dinner Long Awaited always looked at Tashi's plate, and if he thought Tashi had a bigger dumpling or a sweeter peach, he would lean over and grab it.

'One day when Long Awaited whisked a sugar bun from under his nose, Tashi laughed, "You are just like someone I know."

'"Who?"

'"My Uncle Tiki Pu."

'Tashi was soon even dreading walks
down to the village because of the way
Long Awaited barged into shops, sneered at
the goods and took whatever he liked without
paying for it. The shopkeepers were too
frightened of the General to say a word.

'One morning the castle was wakened by a great commotion in the courtyard outside. Two covered carts were rumbling through the gates and when the boys ran to the window they saw young men in red and yellow costumes unloading boxes and poles.

'"Hurrah, the rope walkers have come!" cried Long Awaited. "Come and see."

'During the morning the rope walkers were busy getting ready for the show. They fastened one end of a long rope to a wall above a window on the General's wing of the castle. The other end was taken across the courtyard and fixed to a hook above Long Awaited's bedroom window.

'Tashi gasped. "Are they going to walk that rope? It must be thirty metres high! I hope they've had a lot of practise … Don't they use a safety net?"

'"They do have a net in their cart but my father thinks it's more exciting without one."

'By two o'clock a large crowd from the village and the castle had gathered in the courtyard. The troupe played some favourite country tunes, finishing with a thrilling drum roll.

'Everyone looked up at Long Awaited's window. A figure had climbed up and was standing on the windowsill.

'The crowd cheered as he stepped out onto the rope and made a little bow. "How can he *do* that?" a child whispered. "It looks like magic," breathed a woman to her husband as she watched the young man walk along the rope.

'When he reached the window on the other side, another rope walker started out, this time juggling three glass balls that glittered like rainbows as he threw them up into the sunlight and caught them. He was followed by another who did a little dance halfway across.

'Tashi thought they were the bravest, cleverest people he had ever seen. How many hours and months and years would they have had to practise to become so magnificent? He wondered if they had started with a wooden plank as he and Lotus Blossom had done, balancing it on rocks just a few inches above the ground. He wondered if he would ever get close enough to speak to them. That night at dinner he wanted only to talk about them, but Long Awaited was strangely quiet.

'The next morning the boy couldn't be found. Guards were sent looking for him, and all the servants left their cooking and gardening, washing and dusting to search for him.

'Tashi wondered if Long Awaited was playing hide and seek. Before he went to look, he put on his magic shoes. Taking great galloping leaps he sped around the castle and

forest, searching in all the boy's favourite places. He even ran, quick as the wind, all the way down to the cave at the river. The boy wasn't there. But of course! Long Awaited could never wait long enough to be found – he always dashed out before Tashi had counted to twenty!

'A shout from the courtyard made everyone come running. When Tashi arrived he saw that they were all looking up at Long Awaited's bedroom window. And there he was, standing on his windowsill, holding a long pole across his chest just as the first rope walkers had done.

'"No, no, no, go back!" Tashi cried, pointing wildly at the window behind him. But Long Awaited gave Tashi a confident smile, and moved out onto the rope. The crowd was still. There was not a sound as the boy took his first step. And then another.

'A gust of wind and the rope swayed a little. The smile left Long Awaited's face and his lips trembled. He froze. His face was white. Desperate, he looked down at Tashi and mouthed the words, "Help me!"

'Tashi cupped his mouth with his hands. In his loudest voice he shouted, "Look straight ahead, keep your eyes in front of you!"

'Just at that moment a crow's cry cracked through the sky and Long Awaited wobbled. Dropping his pole, he grabbed at the window behind him. In his terror his foot slipped off the rope and he lunged back, missing the window. His hand caught the rope instead, fingers frantically scrabbling to keep hold. With both hands he clung there, swinging in the icy air.

94

'"I'm coming!" cried Tashi. He knew what he had to do. His toes wriggled deep into his magic shoes and he crouched down, giving himself extra bounce to spring up higher than ever before. In a blink he'd bounded up the wall of the house and slipped inside the window.

'But now Long Awaited was hanging from just a single hand. Tashi could see the knuckles whitening, loosening. He swung crazily for one second, two, three. Only his fingertips were gripping the rope when Tashi reached across, one foot hooked around the windowsill. He grabbed the boy by the arm, pulling him closer until he could grasp both shoulders. Long Awaited nearly strangled him as Tashi dragged what seemed like the heaviest package in the world back through the window and onto the bedroom floor.

'For a moment they clung together, trembling. A shaft of sunlight lit up dancing dust motes. In the quiet, both boys watched them glittering.

'Finally, Tashi smiled. "Well, Long Awaited, I must say that since living here with you, there have not been many dull moments."

'That night, after Long Awaited had been scolded, he came to Tashi's room and sat down. "Thank you, Tashi, for saving me," he said. "I've been thinking, you probably miss your family and village a great deal, don't you?"

'Tashi's heart leapt. "Yes, I do."

'"Well, my father is going to send me to school. He thinks I need more than one boy to keep me busy, so since you've saved my life he's agreed that you can go home to your family. Does that make you happy?"

'Tashi beamed. "Yes, very," he said. Still, he was curious. "How do you feel about my going away?"

'Long Awaited shrugged. "Well, I'd rather you were here to play with me when I'm home from school, but – perhaps you would think that was a bit selfish?" They both laughed.

'"Anyway," said Long Awaited comfortably, "I can always send for you if I need you."

'Once he'd been given permission to leave General Zeng's castle, Tashi didn't waste a minute. He jumped into his magic shoes and set off for home, laughing joyfully as he bounded over creeks and winding roads and fields of flowering thunder god vines.

'Tashi found his front door on the latch as usual; he quietly pushed it open. A babble of voices was coming from the kitchen. Aha, visitors! He crept down the hall and peeped in. Family and friends were crowded around the table.

'"Are you sure you told us everything you saw that night, Tiki Pu?"

'"How many times do I have to say it?" growled Tiki Pu. "It was dark and sudden. All I know is that three big ruffians jumped from behind some bushes and knocked me out with a club. When I woke up Tashi was gone."

'"And I keep saying it seems very strange that your cuts and scratches didn't appear until the next day," muttered Lotus Blossom.

'Tiki Pu shrugged his shoulders and wriggled uncomfortably in his chair. He turned his head and suddenly his jaw dropped.

A look of horror stole over his face as his eyes fell on the figure standing in the doorway.

"'Tashi!" he gasped. Everybody swivelled to look and a great shout went up as they scrambled over to hug and touch and clap Tashi on the back. All except Tiki Pu. He stood back, as the egg noodles he'd had for breakfast came up into his mouth and he swallowed them down again. Finally he pushed himself forward and forced a welcoming smile across his face.

"'Tashi!" he gasped. "H-How glad we are t-to see you, back s-safe and sound." Tiki Pu gazed imploringly at Tashi.

'For several minutes Tashi stared back, watching his uncle stew and sweat. Then he turned back to his family, who were begging him to tell the story of what happened to him.

'"Well, it was like this..." he began and, just as Tiki Pu had done, he told them all about General Zeng and Long Awaited, leaving out any mention of Tiki Pu's part in it. Tiki Pu was just heaving a sigh of relief when Tashi added thoughtfully, "The only thing I haven't been able to figure out is why General Zeng should have done such a thing."

'Tiki Pu caught his breath. Tashi gave him another steely glance, but said no more.

'It was later, when they were alone, that Tiki Pu learned the price he was to pay for his crime.

'"You will find a new place to live, Tiki Pu,' said Tashi. 'And then you will go to Wise-as-an-Owl and offer to gather the seeds of the thunder god vines for his medicines. And by the time you have filled three bucketsful, the poppy seeds should be ready to collect and the gingko – and then you will do whatever Wise-as-an-Owl needs you to do until the summer is over. You will be very busy – too busy to cause any more trouble for my family. And if you slack off in any way, you will find that my memory of the terrible deal you made with General Zeng will come back and you will be spurned by the village forever."

'Lotus Blossom, who had stayed behind when the others had left, came back into

the room. "Well, I think you let him off too lightly," she growled.

'Tashi joined her at the table. "Keeping in mind that, although Tiki Pu is a disgrace to the family, he is, after all, *our* disgrace. What do you think I should do with him?"

'Lotus Blossom giggled. "Let's see ... we could ..."

'They whispered together for some time suggesting more and more impossible punishments until they were quite exhausted with laughter. They finally settled on a satisfactory penalty, which seems to have worked because everybody agrees that from that day forward, Tiki Pu is a changed man.'

Mum scratched her hives thoughtfully. 'Maybe Aunty Fullpot isn't quite so bad after all.'

'*No one* would be, compared with that Uncle Tiki Pu,' said Dad. And the next time they were invited over to Aunty Fullpot's to mend the fence and clean the gutters and oh, to have afternoon tea, Dad didn't say they were busy. But he still ate too much.

Meet Tashi – he's as brave as he's clever, and he tells the best stories ever. Giants, ghosts, witches and war lords are no match for Tashi!

Eight bestselling stories about Tashi's daring adventures in each volume!

Learn the alphabet, how to count and the names of colours as you journey through Tashi's world filled with mythical creatures, wild adventures and magic.

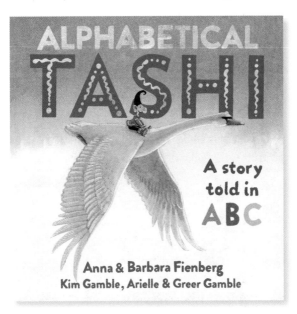

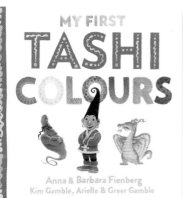

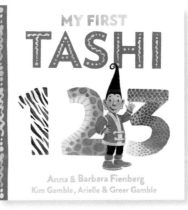

When Anna Fienberg was little, her mother, Barbara, read lots of stories to her. At bedtime they would travel to secret places in the world, through books. Now Anna and Barbara write the Tashi stories together, making up all kinds of daredevil adventures and tricky characters for him to face. Kim Gamble has done the wonderful illustrations for the Tashi stories.

Which Tashi adventures have you read?

Tashi
Tashi and the Giants
Tashi and the Ghosts
Tashi and the Genie
Tashi and the Baba Yaga
Tashi and the Demons
Tashi and the Big Stinker
Tashi and the Dancing Shoes
Tashi and the Haunted House
Tashi and the Royal Tomb
Tashi Lost in the City
Tashi and the Forbidden Room
Tashi and the Stolen Bus
Tashi and the Mixed-up Monster
Tashi and the Phoenix
Tashi and the Golem
The Amazing Tashi Activity Book
Once Tashi Met a Dragon
There Once Was a Boy Called Tashi
Tashi and the Wicked Magician

Royal Tomb

Village Square

Fields

Baron's House

Mountain of
White Tigers

Cemetery